WE ARE THE SHAPES

For my M & P, Nigel and Shields.
Thank you for giving me the freedom and support to
choose my own path. To Jessica for lighting the way.

Ichabod—I'm yours, always, my little toothless one.
But you are a cat and you cannot read.

For Tadley.

—K.

Brimming with creative inspiration, how-to
projects, and useful information to enrich your
everyday life, quarto.com is a favorite destination
for those pursuing their interests and passions.

© 2022 Quarto Publishing Group USA Inc.
Text and illustration © Kevin Jenner

Kevin Jenner has asserted his right to be identified as the author and illustrator of this work.

First published in 2022 by Happy Yak,
an imprint of The Quarto Group.
100 Cummings Center, Suite 265D
Beverly, MA 01915, USA.
T (978) 282-9590 F (978) 283-2742
www.quarto.com

All rights reserved. No part of this publication may be reproduced, stored in a retrieval
system, or transmitted in any form, or by any means, electrical, mechanical, photocopying,
recording or otherwise, without the prior written permission of the publisher or a licence
permitting restricted copying.

A CIP record for this book is available from the Library of Congress.

ISBN: 978-0-7112-7264-4

Manufactured in Guangdong, China CC052022
9 8 7 6 5 4 3 2 1

WE ARE THE SHAPES

KEVIN JENNER

happy yak

This is a square.

I AM A SQUARE.

And these are the squares.

WE ARE THE
SQUARES!

A square has four sides.
And all four sides are exactly the same.

Squares are quite simple, really.

They don't like things that are different.
Different is odd and squares prefer things to be even.

But THIS is a triangle.

SQUARES ARE REALLY BORING!

Triangles are nothing like squares.

They have three sides and come in different shapes and sizes.

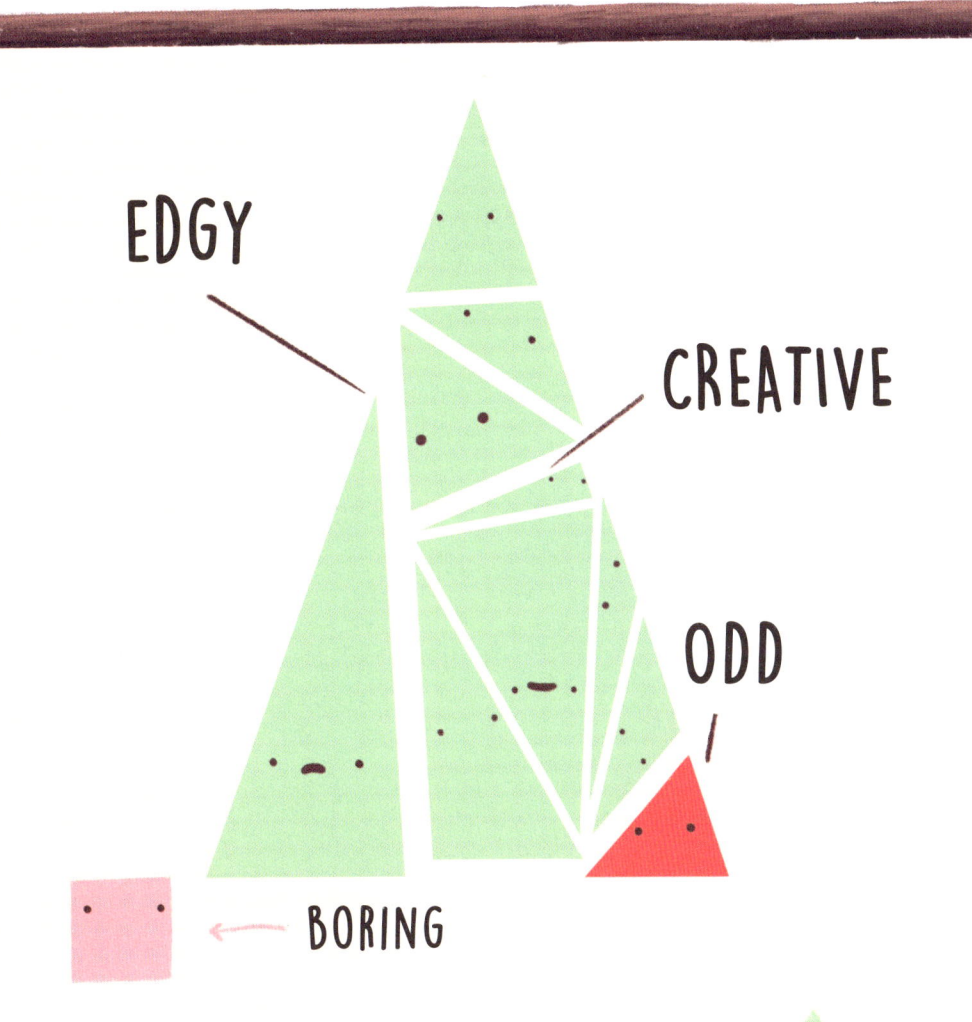

EDGY

CREATIVE

ODD

← BORING

Triangles don't mind being different. Different is fun.

Oh and umm, I forgot to mention that these guys REALLY don't like each other.

Like, not at all.

They fight A LOT. Over anything, really... cats, dogs, their favorite colors, art...

...and games can be a big deal.

Now, this blue guy...
is a circle.

And you see the one thing about circles...

...is that they don't have sides.

But circles are good at turning things around.

HEY! HERE'S A BRIGHT IDEA!

And this circle knows that the squares and triangles could get along—they just need to roll with their differences.

Circle just hopes
that one day...

...the squares and the triangles will realize...

...that together...

...they could achieve anything!

But...

...unfortunately...

GASP!!!

Sometimes ideas don't work. But...

...there are always new ideas.

HEY! SQUARES AND TRIANGLES BOTH LOVE FOOD. MAYBE PIZZA WILL HELP...

(OCTAGONS ARE COMPLICATED. WE'LL LEAVE THEM FOR ANOTHER STORY...)

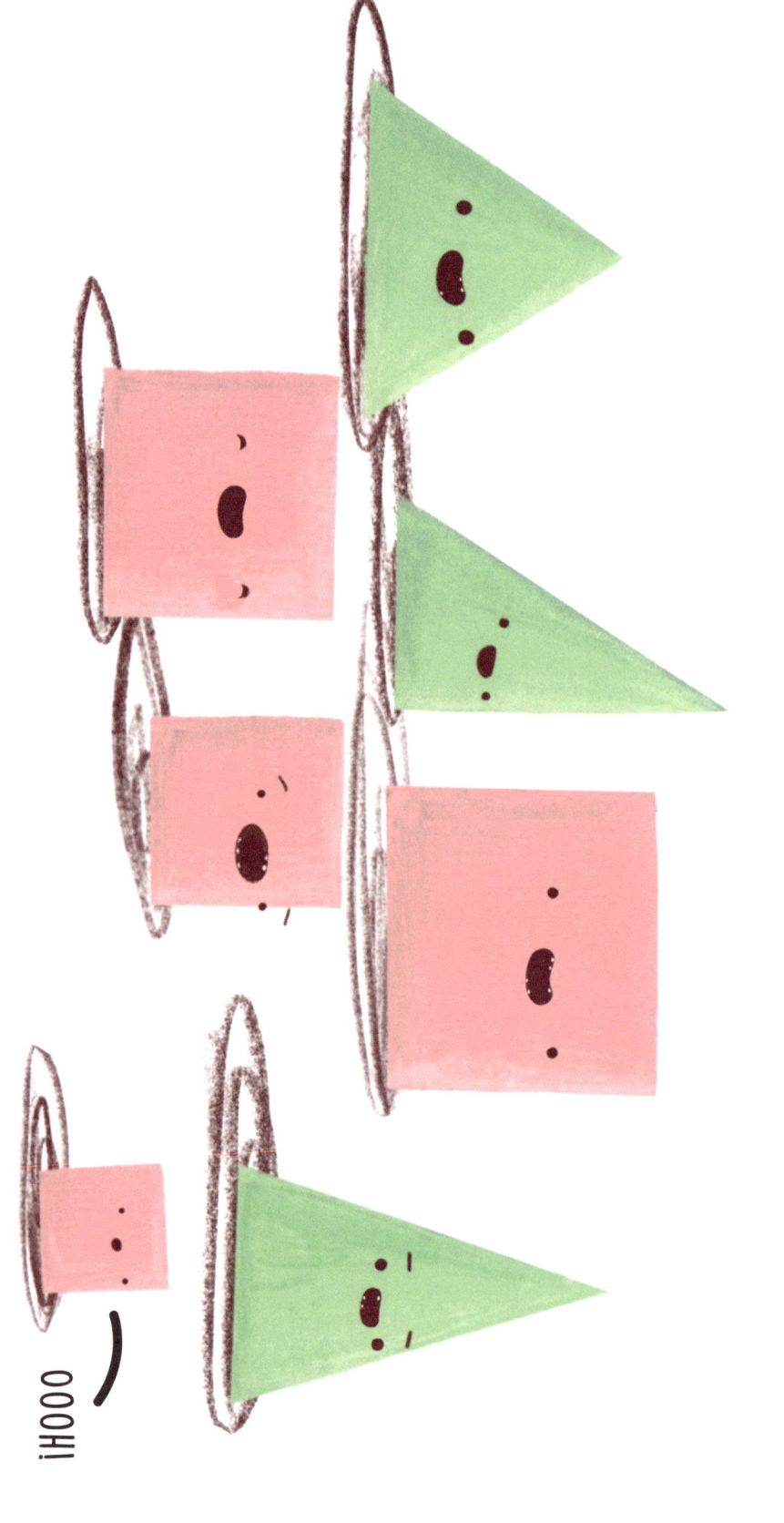

Did I mention circles are good at turning things around?

The end.